NIA'S PUZZLE

A story about the "big picture" perspective.

DR. CANDICE CARMEL WEAVER

Nia's Puzzle
By Dr. Candice Carmel Weaver

Printed in the United States of America
Publisher A. Robins Nest, LLC
ISBN 9781085817547

Illustrated by Andi Triyanta

www.AmberRobinsNestMedia.com

Special thanks to
Thea Monyee' Winkler, Dana Carmel Bell, Lisa Washington, Micah R. Eubanks, Arah Y. Sims, and the many friends and family who provided valuable feedback and encouragement during the process of writing this book.

This book is dedicated to the loves of my life:
James Jr., Myles, and Kamaryn.
My greatest desire for you is not that you live lives free of adversity, but that you enjoy the journey and appreciate the lessons you'll learn along the way.

To my mother and constant cheerleader, Karen Blagmon; from whom I learned faith and fortitude, grace and gumption, humility and humor, and to never, ever, ever give up.

To my best friend and husband, James; from whom I constantly learn
integrity, loyalty, and unconditional love.

And to my dad, Gary Blagmon; my guardian angel, with whom I meet up for advice and laughter every night in my dreams.

"What shall we do tonight,

baby love?"

"Cookies, stories, puzzles?
Or all of the above?"

"All of the above!"
I said with delight.

(I love when my Nana lets me
spend the night.)

With cookies in the oven,
and slippers on my feet,
Nana pulled out a puzzle
and I settled in my seat.

PUZZ

Nana sat at the table, looked at me, and smiled.

"Which story, sweet Nia, would you like me to repeat?"

"A new one today, Nana!"
I replied with a grin
(knowing Nana didn't want to tell an old one again).

"Can you tell me the story
that your Grandma told you
about why things in life
happen the way that they do?"

PUZZLE

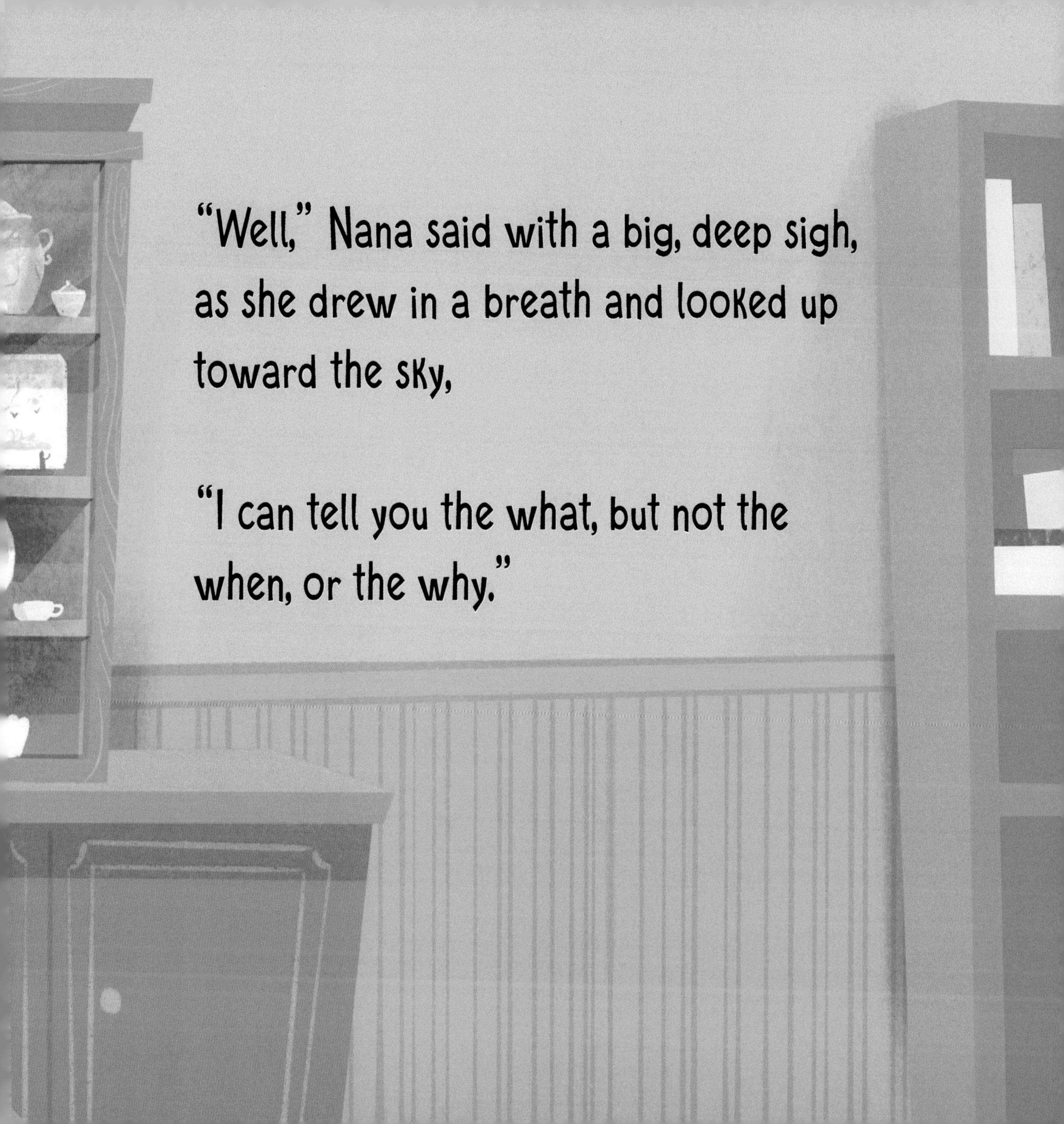

"Well," Nana said with a big, deep sigh, as she drew in a breath and looked up toward the sky,

"I can tell you the what, but not the when, or the why."

"Just like the puzzle
we're working on now,
you'll have to put together life's purpose—
it's up to you to learn how."

"See, we get these pieces one at a time.

Sometimes they're odd—
with no reason or rhyme.

Sometimes it's easy to see where they fit.

Other times, we're confused
about the pieces we get."

"This blue piece you have—
it might be the sea.

But don't jump to conclusions about
where it should be!

It may belong in the sky,
or on a flower in the dirt.

It could be someone's eye,
or the color of their shirt."

"As you grow up,
you'll never know what
piece you'll get.

Some of them won't
make sense, which may
cause you to fret.

Your job is to take that piece
and try to be smart,
while using your brain
and also your heart."

"If the piece doesn't fit
where you believe it belongs,
it's probably 'cause the picture
you envisioned was wrong.

Don't get frustrated, Nia.
Set it aside, in that case.

Don't force it where it doesn't
easily fall into place."

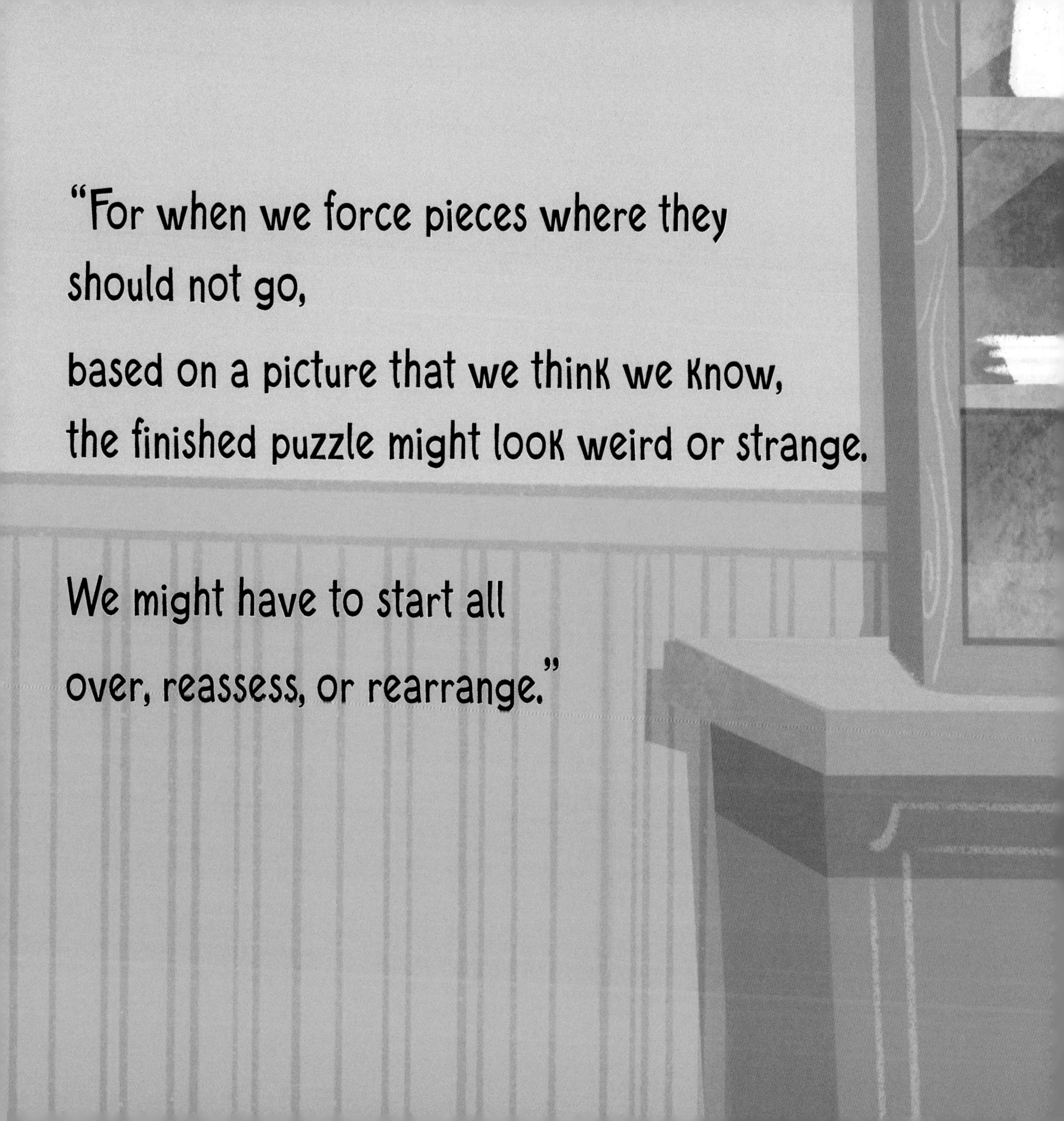

"For when we force pieces where they should not go,

based on a picture that we think we know,

the finished puzzle might look weird or strange.

We might have to start all over, reassess, or rearrange."

"As you put together your pieces, Nia,
you'll notice in due time,
it gets easier to determine
where they fit in your life.

One day, you'll look back
when your picture's near done
and realize the purpose
of each and every one."

"Some pieces you once thought
had important potential
were part of the background and
much less essential.

And some of the odd pieces you
couldn't stand to see,
add to the big picture
beautifully."

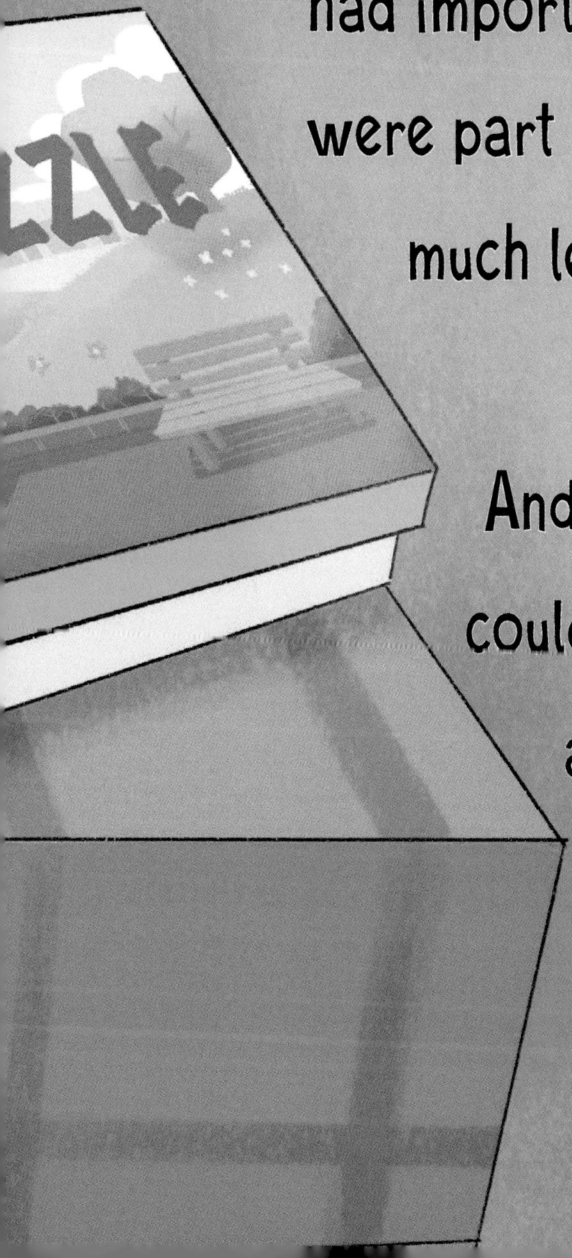

"But Nana, can you tell me NOW
what my big picture will be?"

"Your puzzle's barely started –
so we'll have to wait and see.
Don't rush to put it together;
the fun is in the wait.
Whatever your big picture shows,
I know it will be great!"

"Grandma, can you tell me the
story that your Nana told you,
about why things in life
happen the way that they do?"

To be continued...

Dr. Candice Carmel Weaver is an alumnus of U.C. Berkeley, The Johns Hopkins University, Dartmouth College, and Touro University. She is a board certified Family Medicine physician who has traveled the world in pursuit of happiness, love, and purpose. In her spare time, she enjoys playing the piano, watching and coaching basketball, baking, and spending time with her husband and three children.

Visit the Nia's Puzzle website to learn more about Dr. Weaver's approach to living with resilience through problem-solving, perseverance, and perspective. There, you can download a Discussion Guide for Parents and Teachers to help encourage a healthy dialogue with your children.

www.NiasPuzzle.Com

Made in the USA
Columbia, SC
24 August 2019